April 25, 2023

TODAY, FOLKS,

WE'RE MAKING

WOOFLES.

MAKING A *career* OUT OF

Fetch

SINCE 2012

STOP
IN THE NAME OF THE
PAW

THAT'S WHAT *I think* **OF** YOUR "TEAM SPIRIT," *Susan.*

THERE'S **NOTHING** *wrong* WITH MY BEDSIDE *manner!*

ME
LEAVING
THE OFFICE
ON A
FRIDAY

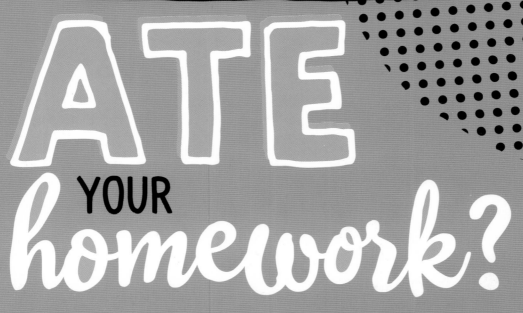

DON'T TELL ME...
THE DOG
ATE
YOUR
homework?

I NEED SOME SPACE.

PREFERABLY AWAY FROM

YOU!

YEAH, I'M INTO FITNESS:

FITNESS

WHOLE

BISCUIT

IN MY

MOUTH.

Yummy

WHAT DO YOU MEAN,

you're giving

VANESSA *the*

PROMOTION?!

HAVE YOU ACTUALLY

READ MY

LAB

report?

WHEN THEY TOLD ME TO

"SIT and WAIT,"

THIS IS NOT WHAT
I HAD IN MIND.

DON'T *you*
THINK I'VE *tried*
TURNING IT
OFF (AND) ON
AGAIN?

IT'S A

DOG eat DOG

WORLD.

SHERLOCK BONES

DETECTIVE

RESIDENT OF

221B BARKER STREET

"Working" FROM home...

IT'S EXHAUSTING.

YOU SAY "ANNUAL LEAVE."

I SAY "Caribbean cruise."

DID I JUST HEAR dog biscuits?

BEING FABULOUS IS A full-time job!

CONGRATULATIONS!

WE'RE OFFERING YOU A

permanent

position

THIS WEEK I'M
MOSTLY
WORKING
ON MY
PAWSTURE

NO PAIN,

NO GAIN,

people!

FEEL THE BURN.

HERE'S ONE I WROTE ABOUT

DOG BISCUITS.

THESE **BOOTS** WERE MADE FOR *walkies*

DO YOU WANT *one* LICK OF PAINT OR *two*?

YOU could AT LEAST TRY to smile FOR THE CAMERA, Philip.

WHEN YOU

OVERSLEEP,

AND ONLY HAVE

FOUR MINUTES

TO GET TO THE FOOD BOWL IN TIME.

THESE OPTICIAN JOKES JUST GET CORNEA AND CORNEA

DRESS
FOR THE JOB YOU WANT
NOT THE JOB YOU HAVE